You, of ~~...~~ on land, you are warm and dry. ~~...~~ you are on a small boat in an angry sea, with salt water flying into your face and the wind screaming in your ears. For us it is easy not to be afraid; this is only a book. But for Grace Darling it was no story. It was a very real, cold, wild night when she fought with the sea, and was not afraid.

OXFORD BOOKWORMS LIBRARY

True Stories

Grace Darling

Stage 2 (700 headwords)

Series Editor: Jennifer Bassett
Founder Editor: Tricia Hedge
Activities Editors: Jennifer Bassett and Alison Baxter

TIM VICARY

Grace Darling

OXFORD UNIVERSITY PRESS

OXFORD
UNIVERSITY PRESS

Great Clarendon Street, Oxford OX2 6DP

Oxford University Press is a department of the University of Oxford.
It furthers the University's objective of excellence in research, scholarship,
and education by publishing worldwide in

Oxford New York

Auckland Cape Town Dar es Salaam Hong Kong Karachi
Kuala Lumpur Madrid Melbourne Mexico City Nairobi
New Delhi Shanghai Taipei Toronto

With offices in

Argentina Austria Brazil Chile Czech Republic France Greece
Guatemala Hungary Italy Japan Poland Portugal Singapore
South Korea Switzerland Thailand Turkey Ukraine Vietnam

OXFORD and OXFORD ENGLISH are registered trade marks of
Oxford University Press in the UK and in certain other countries

ISBN-13: 978 0 19 422974 6
ISBN-10: 0 19 422974 2

Printed in Hong Kong

ACKNOWLEDGEMENTS

CONTENTS

STORY INTRODUCTION   i

1   The *Forfarshire*   1

2   The Lighthouse   6

3   In the Engine Room   10

4   Nothing to See   13

5   The Shipwreck   16

6   Out of the Window   19

7   On Harker's Rock   24

8   The Worst Sea this Year   25

9   Angel in the Storm   30

10   Too Many People   32

GLOSSARY   41

ACTIVITIES: Before Reading   44

ACTIVITIES: While Reading   45

ACTIVITIES: After Reading   48

ABOUT THE AUTHOR   52

ABOUT BOOKWORMS   53

1

The Forfarshire

Daniel Donovan was a passenger on the *Forfarshire*. He stood on the deck of the ship, and looked at the sea. It was difficult to stand on the deck, because the wind was so strong. The ship was moving up and down uncomfortably and Daniel felt ill. Then a big wave hit the side of the ship, and salt water flew into his face.

'The wind is getting stronger,' said a passenger beside him. He was a tall, dark man with a black coat – Mr Robb, a churchman. 'And it's getting darker, too.'

'Yes,' said Daniel. 'I can't see the land now.' He looked to the west, but he could see no land, no lights. Only water – big grey waves with white tops, which went up and down, up and down.

'But the *Forfarshire* is a good modern ship,' said Mr Robb. 'Nothing can happen to a new ship like this. Listen to those fine strong engines!'

Daniel looked down at the big paddle wheel on the side of the ship. It went round and round, down under the white water, and up again . . . under the water, and up. Then he looked up at the black smoke which came from the *Forfarshire*'s funnel.

'Yes,' he said. 'They're good, strong engines.' But he was not really sure. He was an engineer, so he knew about

engines. Sometimes the *Forfarshire*'s engines made strange noises, and the paddle wheels went round slowly. Then there was a crash, and they went quickly again. Daniel was not happy.

A sea bird flew low across the white tops of the big, grey waves. Daniel watched it, and felt wind and rain on his face. Then a door opened behind him, and a woman screamed.

'Simon, come back! Come back at once!'

Daniel looked behind him, and saw a small boy. He was

Sometimes the Forfarshire's *engines made strange noises, and the paddle wheels went round slowly.*

running across the deck. He was only three or four years old, and the wind was much too strong for him. He fell over on the deck and began to cry. Then another big wave hit the side of the ship. The white water came over the side and carried the boy along the deck.

'Help!' the woman screamed. 'Save my child!'

Daniel put out a hand and caught the boy's coat. Then he carried him quickly back to his mother.

'Quick! Get back in, out of the wind, woman!' he shouted. He hurried through the door and closed it with a crash. 'It's too dangerous for children out there!'

'Yes, I know,' the woman said. 'Come here, Simon!' She sat down and held the boy with one arm. She had another child in her other arm – a little girl, about one or two years old. 'Thank you, sir,' she said.

The ship moved up and down very quickly, and Daniel sat down beside the woman. She smiled at him, but she looked very white and ill.

'I'm Daniel Donovan,' he said. 'What's your name?'

'Mary Dawson,' she said. 'This is my son Simon, and my daughter Sarah.'

'Isn't your husband with you?'

'No,' she said. 'He's in Scotland. We're going home to see him. It's good we're in a strong, modern ship.'

'Yes,' said Daniel. Then for a few seconds he said nothing. It was quiet in this room. Much quieter than outside.

'Mr Donovan,' said Mrs Dawson suddenly. 'What's

happened to the engines? I can't hear them now. Can you?'

Daniel listened. 'My God,' he thought. 'She's right! The engines have stopped!' He could hear the noise of the wind and the sea, but not the engines. 'You're right, Mrs Dawson,' he said. He stood up, and ran to the door. 'Excuse me. I . . .' But then he opened the door, and his words were lost in the wind.

Outside, he looked up at the ship's funnel. There was no smoke above it. He looked over the side of the ship, at the big paddle wheels. He watched them for two minutes, but they did not move. And all the time the big

'What's happened to the engines?' said Mrs Dawson suddenly.

grey waves lifted the *Forfarshire* up and down, and white water blew over the deck.

'What's happening?' screamed Mr Robb. 'Why aren't we moving?'

'The engines have broken down!' shouted Donovan. 'This isn't a sailing ship – it can't move without its engines!'

A big wave hit the side of the paddle wheel and sent white water over their heads. Some sailors were trying to put up a small sail, but the wind blew it out of their hands, away across the sea into the night.

'There are women and children on this ship,' shouted Mr Robb. 'It's nearly dark, and the weather is getting worse. What can we do?'

Daniel looked at him. 'I don't know, my friend,' he shouted back. 'I can't do anything. Why not ask God – you're a churchman! Perhaps He'll send an angel to save us!'

2

The Lighthouse

When the engines stopped, the *Forfarshire* was about five kilometres east of St Abbs Head, in Scotland. The ship was travelling north, from Hull to Dundee. But the wind came from the north, so the *Forfarshire*, without her engines, began to go south again, back to England. It was dark, and the wind was very strong.

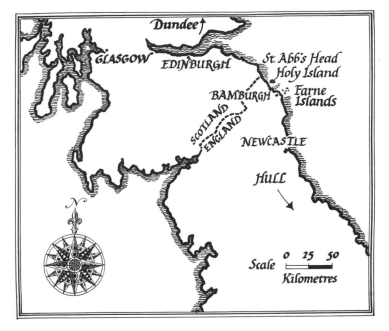

About thirty kilometres south-east of St Abbs Head is a group of small rocky islands not far from the mainland. These are the Farne Islands. On one of them, Longstone Island, there is a lighthouse. There were three people in the lighthouse that night – William Darling, his wife Thomasin, and their daughter Grace. Grace's brothers were usually there too, but that night they were in Bamburgh, on the mainland.

At seven o'clock that night, William Darling went up the long stairs of the lighthouse to light the big oil lantern. Grace went with him. William Darling was a thin, strong man about fifty years old. He moved quickly and quietly. He had a candle in his hand. Sometimes he turned to talk to Grace, and the candlelight lit up the big brown eyes in his kind, old face.

Grace was a young woman about twenty-two years old. She was not very tall or strong. She had big brown eyes like her father, and soft brown hair. She carried an oil can in one hand, and held the side of her long skirts with the other hand. She smiled at her father while they talked.

At the top of the lighthouse Grace and her father came into a small room. This room had no walls – just big windows all around. The noise of the wind and rain was terrible here, and they had to shout to hear each other.

Grace put oil in the big lantern in the middle of the room, and William lit it. When the lantern was burning, the big silver mirrors began to move slowly around it. William Darling and his daughter stood and watched them. The rain crashed against the windows, and the wind screamed like an animal in the night.

'God help the poor sailors to see this light,' shouted William. 'It's as dark as death out there. No moon, no stars – nothing but wind and rain and wild white water.'

'Let us pray there are no ships near the rocks,' shouted Grace. 'The storm will wreck any ship that comes near them tonight.'

'That's true, lass,' said William. 'But we can do no more now. Let's go down to supper.'

The father and daughter went slowly down the dark, narrow stairs to the kitchen. Grace's mother, Thomasin, was putting the supper on the table. She was a white-

'God help the poor sailors to see this light.'

haired woman of sixty-five.

'Did you see anything?' she asked.

'No, my love, nothing,' William answered. 'Only the rain on the windows.'

'Thank God,' she said. 'You couldn't help anyone tonight, William. If there is a shipwreck, you can do nothing. The boys aren't here.'

'But, mother,' Grace said. 'Father has to try to save people. It's his job. He can't leave them to die.'

'Grace, no man could row a boat by himself in this wild sea,' said Thomasin. 'So let us thank God that there are no poor ships near us, on this terrible night.'

'Yes, Grace, let us thank God for that,' said William. And so the three people sat quietly around their table in the warm kitchen, and put their hands together to pray. In the black night outside, the wind screamed, and the big waves crashed against the rocks, again and again and again.

3

In the Engine Room

'Mr Donovan!'
'Yes.'

'The captain wants to see you. You're an engineer, aren't you? Come this way, please.' The sailor opened a door and Daniel went quickly inside. They went down some stairs. He opened another door, and a great cloud of steam came out. Daniel followed the young sailor into the room. It was very hot in here, and there were clouds of steam everywhere. A tall, red-faced man came up to him.

'Mr Donovan? My name's Humble, Captain Humble. We need you, sir. You're an engineer, I understand. One of these engines has already stopped, and the other is working very badly. There's too much steam in this room, sir, and not . . .'

A big wave hit the ship with a terrible crash and Daniel, Captain Humble and the young sailor held onto the wall. Daniel saw a big man in a blue coat, and shouted to him.

'Are you the ship's engineer?'

'Yes!' The man looked angry, tired, and frightened.

'What's the matter? Why has this engine stopped?'

'Why? Because it's too old, of course! Look here! See this? And this . . .' For five minutes the two engineers moved around in the steam and smoke, and looked at the big engines.

'See? It's broken here, and here! How can I mend it now, in the middle of a storm? Can you do that, sir?'

Daniel shook his head. He was angry and frightened. 'No, of course I can't! The ship must go back to land!'

The man agreed quickly. 'That's right, that's what I say! But you tell Captain Humble that! He says this a new, modern ship, so it can go anywhere, in any weather! Our rich passengers want to go to Scotland, so that's where we're going, he says! But it's too dangerous and . . .'

The man stopped when Captain Humble came near. 'Well, Mr Donovan? Can you help us? Do you know more about engines than this stupid engineer here? He says he can do nothing, and we must go back to Hull, because of a small storm! But I'm sure . . .'

'He's right, Captain Humble!' shouted Daniel. 'I can do nothing for these engines here, in this storm! They're too old, and this one is broken in three places! We must go

*'These engines are too old, and this one is broken
in three places!'*

back to land, Captain, or we will all drown! I cannot help
you!'

'Gaaaaaargh!' The captain pushed Daniel angrily away
from him. 'Then get out of my way, Mr Donovan – you're
no good to me! Get back to the women and children!'

Daniel went quickly to the door, and up the stairs to
the wind and rain outside. But he was a badly frightened
man. His hands were shaking, and it was hard for him to
stand in the terrible screaming wind. Above his head, two
sailors were putting up a small sail. 'That's no good,' he
thought. 'It's too small for a big ship like this. Without
engines, we can do nothing.'

He stared out to sea, but he could see nothing – only
the white tops of the great black waves, and the black
clouds above. No stars, no moon. But – far away to the

south west – there was a little light flashing. On . . . off
. . . on . . . off. It went behind a wave, and then came back
again, like a star in the night sky, far away.

But it was coming nearer. Nearer all the time.

4

Nothing to See

It was half past two in the morning. In the lighthouse,
Grace was asleep in her room. It was a small, tidy room,
with white walls. Her dress was on the back of the door,
and her other clothes were on a chair by the bed. There
were some books on a desk, and some sea-birds' eggs on a
table.

Someone knocked at the door. 'Grace!' her father's
voice called. 'Wake up, lass. I need you to help me.'

'What is it, father?' She got up quickly, and opened the
door. William Darling stood there with a candle in his
hand. He was wearing his big black coat and heavy boots,
and his hat was pulled down over his ears. His face was
tired, and wet with rain.

'The storm is worse. The wind is coming from the north
now, and it's stronger. We shall have to go outside and
tie the boat down, or we shall lose it!'

'All right. I'll be down in a minute.' Quickly, Grace
closed the door and put her clothes on. She often got up
in the night. There was always work on a lighthouse, and

the sea did not wait for morning. A minute later, she ran downstairs to the kitchen, put a coat over her thin dress, tied her hair under her hat, and followed her father out into the night.

The wind nearly lifted her off her feet. It was strong, black, hard, and wet. She opened her mouth to call to her father, but the words blew away into the night. Her coat and dress blew out behind her like paper, and the rain hit her face, like small stones.

She walked slowly after her father, to the boathouse. Her father was carrying a small lantern, and in its light Grace saw a great wave of white water. It broke against the rock in front of the boathouse, and white water crashed against the boathouse doors. William shouted something to Grace but she could not hear him – the sounds of the wind and the sea were too loud, too terrible.

In the boathouse, she helped her father tie the boat down to the rock. They tied down the oars, too, so that nothing could move them. Then they ran outside and carried everything into the kitchen – their chickens, their fishing things. Nothing could stay outside on a night like this.

Before they went back in, Grace stared out into the night. The light from the top of the lighthouse flashed out over the water, and for thirty seconds she could see very well. One after another, the big, black waves came out of the darkness – waves ten, twenty metres high! When they hit the rock there was a huge crash, and white water flew everywhere, thirty, forty metres up over the Longstone rock.

Grace stared out, over the waves, past the rocks and islands. But – thank God! – she could see no lights, no ships. No ship could live in that sea tonight.

'Grace! Come on in, lass!' Her father held the door open behind her. She went in quickly, and he closed the door behind them. Her mother had warm drinks ready for them.

'Go to bed now, father,' Grace said. 'You've had no

A great wave broke against the rock, and white water crashed against the boathouse doors.

sleep yet tonight. I'll watch the light now, and mother can come up at five.'

'All right, lass,' he said. William was very tired. He went upstairs with his wife, and in two minutes they were asleep.

Grace finished her drink quickly, and changed out of her wet clothes. Then she went up alone to the room with the big windows at the top of the lighthouse. The wild wind screamed, and shook the glass.

It was half past three in the morning.

5

The Shipwreck

In the passengers' sitting room on the *Forfarshire* Mrs Dawson looked unhappily at Daniel, Mr Robb, and two other men – Thomas Buchanan and James Kelly. Her two children were crying in her arms. 'I'm so frightened. Do you think we're going to die? What can we do, Mr Donovan, without the engines?'

'Not much, Mrs Dawson,' said Daniel slowly. 'But there are some islands, south of here, called the Farne Islands. They are very near. I've seen the lighthouse flashing on them. I think the captain is trying to go into the quieter water between the islands and the mainland. I . . . I'll go outside again, to see how near the lighthouse is. I'll come back and tell you.'

Daniel got up and went out into the night. It was raining hard now, and the wind was screaming from the back of the ship. He stared into the dark. He could see nothing in the west. Where was the light? He walked carefully across the ship, to the other side. Suddenly he fell on the wet deck, and he caught the side of the ship with his hands. Then he looked up, and a light flashed into his eyes. There it was – the lighthouse, only three hundred metres away, to the north!

'But this is wrong!' he thought. 'We're too close! Much too close! I must tell the captain!'

He stood up and began to run along the deck. But there in front of him, a great mountain of white water flew into the sky . . . ten . . . twenty metres above the ship.

'Rocks!' screamed Daniel. 'Rocks! There are rocks in front of us, rocks all round! Captain! CAPTAIN!'

The captain was already shouting at the sailors, and the ship was turning, turning to the west, away from the light. But it was too late. There was a great crash, and Daniel and all the sailors fell to the deck. Then another crash . . . and another. The waves lifted the *Forfarshire* and threw it onto the rock, like a child playing with a toy.

Daniel held onto a rope, and stared into the dark. The light flashed again from the lighthouse. Then he looked back along the ship. People were running out onto the deck, and screaming.

Then another very big wave hit the ship. White water flew everywhere, and fell on Daniel like stones. He heard

White water flew everywhere, and fell on Daniel like stones.

a terrible crash, and more water fell on him. He opened his eyes, and looked back along the ship.

But there was nothing there.

Nothing but black water, and more waves. The ship was broken in two, and the back of the ship, with the captain and all the rich passengers, was not there.

A voice shouted into the wind. 'God help us! Save us from the sea, oh God!' The door of the passengers' room was broken. But there were still some people inside the room – Mr Robb, Mrs Dawson and her two children, Mr Buchanan, and James Kelly. Mr Robb was praying loudly.

Daniel went carefully back along the deck to the broken door. He put out his hand to touch it, and then a wall of white water hit the ship, and he could see nothing.

6

Out of the Window

At twenty to five that morning, Grace felt a hand on her face. It was her mother. Grace was nearly asleep. The wind was screaming and shaking the big windows, and Thomasin Darling had to shout.

'Go to bed, Grace! It's nearly morning. I'll look after the lantern now.'

'All right, mother.' Grace got up slowly and went downstairs to her bedroom. It was much quieter in her room because of the strong stone walls. She looked at the birds' eggs on her table, the books on the desk near the bed. The bed looked warm and comfortable. She smiled, and began to get undressed.

A little grey light was coming in through the window. 'It's nearly morning,' she thought. 'I'll look at the sea, before I go to sleep.'

She walked to the window and looked out. But she could see nothing, because of the salt and rain on the glass. 'It doesn't matter,' she thought. 'I'm too tired. I'll go to bed.'

It was much quieter in her room because of the strong stone walls.

But before she went to bed, she prayed. And when she prayed, she heard a voice in her head. *'Go to the window, Grace,'* it said. *'Go and look out.'*

So she got up, went to the window, and opened it. The wind blew strongly into the room. It blew her hair across her face, and some books fell on the floor. In the grey morning light, Grace looked out across the sea.

Most of the rocks and small islands were under water. Big white waves were breaking over them. The sea was wild, frightening, terrible. Grace looked, and felt cold. She could not remember a storm as bad as this. She thought of her warm bed, and began to close the window.

Then she saw the ship.

It was a big ship, on Harker's Rock, about three hundred metres away to the south west. A very big ship, but it was broken in two, with white water breaking all over it. Grace could not see it very well, because of the rain and the sea.

'Father! Father! Come quick!' She ran out of the room, down the stairs to her parents' bedroom. 'Come quick! There's a ship on Harker's Rock! A big one – a passenger ship! It's broken in two!'

William Darling was out of bed in a second. He put on his boots and coat and followed Grace up the stairs. 'Did you see any people?'

'No, father. But it's difficult to see anything in this wild sea.'

Her father took a telescope from his pocket and stared

out of Grace's window at the wreck of the *Forfarshire*. He
looked for a long time, then said: 'I can see no one, but
my eyes are old. You look, lass.'

Grace stared carefully through the telescope. White
water crashed over the wreck. Sometimes the ship moved
on the rock, and sometimes pieces of wood fell off into
the sea. But she saw no people.

'No, father. I think they have all drowned.'

'Poor, poor people.'

'Yes, but it's a good thing too, William.' Grace's
mother was in the room now, and she was looking out of
the window with her husband and daughter.

'Why is that, Thomasin?' William asked her.

'Why? Because the boys aren't here, William. You
couldn't take a boat out in that wild sea alone. No one
could. If there are people alive on that ship now, you
cannot save them, William.'

'I could go with him, mother,' said Grace quietly.

'Not in a sea like that, Grace,' her mother said.

Her father said nothing.

'We mustn't stop looking,' said Grace. 'If there is
someone alive, we can't just leave them to die.'

And so, for the next two hours, Grace and her parents
watched the wreck of the *Forfarshire* through the
telescope. Slowly, daylight came. But they saw no people
. . . only rain, and waves, and a broken ship in the wild
angry sea.

'If there are people alive on that ship now, you cannot save them, William.'

7

On Harker's Rock

There were twelve people on Harker's Rock. Daniel Donovan was with Mrs Dawson and her children, and there were eight other people near them. The wreck of the *Forfarshire* was behind them, between them and the lighthouse.

They were nearly dead with wet and cold. Every two minutes, white water fell on them. Daniel had lost his coat, and the wind cut through his thin shirt like a knife. His hands and legs were red with blood. Mrs Dawson was crying and sat with her arms around her two small children. Mr Robb prayed in a loud voice without stopping. Thomas Buchanan and the other men sat together, too cold to move. One man had a broken leg.

The waves got bigger, and the people on the rock moved closer together. After half an hour Mr Robb, the churchman, stopped praying. Daniel looked at him. He was lying on the rock, his face white and cold. His eyes were open, but he did not see Daniel's hand in front of his face. He was dead.

'We'll all be dead soon,' shouted Thomas Buchanan angrily. 'No man can live long here, in this wind.'

'Why don't they come from the lighthouse to save us?' shouted James Kelly.

The lighthouse! Daniel remembered it suddenly. 'We must wave to it!' he shouted. 'They can't see us here!

Come up onto the top of the rock! Wave to them!'

Daniel and James Kelly climbed to the top of the rock, but at first the others did not move – they were too cold, too tired, too frightened. Thomas Buchanan had to hit them and push them to the top of the rock.

The wind was very strong there, so it was difficult to stand. They held onto the rock and shouted and waved at the lighthouse as hard as they could.

No one answered. Behind the wild sea and the rain, the lighthouse stood still and quiet. A few minutes later, the light stopped flashing. But they saw nobody. One by one, the men came down from the top of the rock, and sat with their arms around each other, out of the wind. Only Daniel and Thomas Buchanan stayed on top of the rock. They waved and shouted and cried, but they saw no one. Their faces were as cold as death, and salty and wet from the sea.

8

The Worst Sea this Year

Grace saw them first. Her mother was cooking break-fast in the kitchen, and her father was turning off the lantern. Grace was still looking out of her window through the telescope. For a second she saw a man on top of the rock, then she could not see him behind the waves. But a minute later she saw him again – and there were two

They shouted and waved at the lighthouse as hard as they could.

men this time. They stood together and waved wildly.
Then the rain came, and she could see nothing. But
perhaps there were four, or five? She put down the
telescope and called her father.

'Father, come quick! There are men on the rock! They
are still alive!'

William Darling ran into the room. He saw them. He
put down the telescope and looked at his daughter.

'We must go, lass,' he said quietly. 'You and I. We must
take the boat and save them. Will you come?'

'Of course, father,' she said. 'If we don't save them,
who will?'

'That's right, lass.' William Darling looked out of the
window, unhappily. 'I've not seen a worse sea this year.
No boat could come from the mainland in this wind.'

Grace's mother came into the room, and heard him.
'You can't go, William!' she said. 'Grace is only a girl.
Look at that sea! You'll both drown!'

'We have to try, mother!' said Grace angrily. 'Think of
those poor people, alone on that rock. We live on a
lighthouse – it's our job!'

'It's a job for your father and brothers, Grace, not you!
You'll drown! How will that help those men?'

'How will it help them if we do nothing?'

Thomasin Darling looked out of the window again, at
the wild, angry sea. She shook her head. 'Perhaps you'll
get to the rock, Grace,' she said. 'With God's help and the
wind behind you. But you'll never get back against the

wind. Not one man and a girl in a storm like this. Never.'

William Darling took his wife's hands in his. 'Listen to me, Thomasin,' he said. 'There are three or four seamen on that rock. Strong men. They'll help row us back, if we save them.'

'*If* you save them,' said Thomasin. 'And if you don't . . . ?'

At first William Darling did not answer. He looked into his wife's eyes. 'We're going, Thomasin,' he said quietly. 'We have to go. Come down now and help us with the boat.'

Outside, in the terrible wind and the rain, it took them fifteen minutes to get the boat ready. Three times the waves nearly broke the boat on the rock. William got in first, and sat at the front. Grace and her mother held the boat away from the rocks. William got two oars ready, and waited for the next wave.

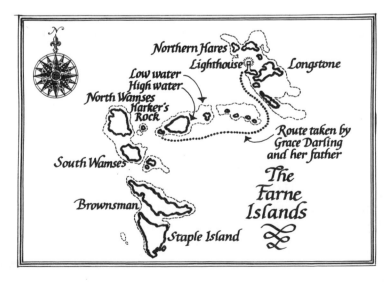

'All right, Grace! Get in *now*!' he shouted.

Grace jumped into the boat, and William pulled hard with the oars. One . . . two . . . three pulls, and then a wave lifted the boat and the oars were pulling at air. But they were away from the rocks. The boat came down between two waves, and Grace quickly got her oars out. They both pulled hard together, but carefully too. They did not want to lose an oar in the wild water. Grace was cold and her dress and hat were wet. She was afraid, but happy and excited too. 'This is what God wants me to do,' she thought. At the top of a wave she could easily see across the Longstone rock to the other side. Then the boat went down between the waves and she could see only mountains of wild water everywhere.

'Pull left! Left!' William shouted. 'We must keep the rocks between us and the worst waves!'

Grace pulled hard at her oars, and watched the waves. 'God will help us save them!' she thought happily. 'I know He will.'

Outside the lighthouse, Thomasin Darling watched the little boat. She saw it for a second, then it went behind a wave, and came up again. 'It's not possible,' she thought. 'No boat can live in a sea like that! Oh God, please – save my husband and daughter!'

She watched and prayed, and the little boat got smaller and smaller on the wild, grey sea.

9

Angel in the Storm

'Help me, Mr Donovan! Please help!'

'How can I help you, woman?' Daniel shouted at Mrs Dawson. 'How can anyone help?' He was too cold, too frightened, too tired. He couldn't think now.

'Please help my children!' cried Mrs Dawson. 'Keep them warm for me – they're so cold!'

Daniel put his arms around the woman and her children. It was true. The children were cold – very cold. Their eyes were open, but they were not moving. He tried to warm them with his hands. He shook them, but they did not move.

'It's no good, woman!' he said. 'No one can . . .'

'They're not dead yet!' screamed Mrs Dawson. 'I know they're not dead!' She looked into her children's faces. 'Wake up, Simon! Sarah! God will save us soon. Please don't die!'

Daniel was tired and angry. 'Don't be stupid, woman!' he shouted at her. 'We're all going to die, don't you understand? No one knows we're here!'

Mrs Dawson stared at him. Her face was wet with rain, and her hair was blowing in her eyes.

'God will send someone!' she said. 'He must! I know He will!'

'Who's He going to send? An angel?' Daniel laughed angrily, and looked at the wild, empty sea.

'We're all going to die!' Daniel shouted. 'No one knows we're here!'

But Mrs Dawson was still screaming. 'Someone *must* come!' she shouted. 'We can't die here! Go to the top of the rock and look again! Tell them about my children!'

'Your children are . . .' But he was afraid to say it. He turned away, angry with himself, and climbed to the top of the rock. The wind screamed in his ears. He looked across to the lighthouse and saw nothing – only waves, and more waves. 'I hate the sea!' he thought. 'It's like a great grey animal with a hundred white teeth. I hate it! It wants to kill us all!'

And then he saw the boat.

He saw it only for a second. It was on top of a white

wave. It went down behind the wave, but then it came up again. Down, and up again. And it was coming nearer! A little boat with two people in it. He held the rock and stared at it. The boat came nearer, and nearer still. Then a great mountain of a wave came, with white angry teeth, and the little boat went down behind it.

'No!' Daniel cried. 'No, please God! No!'

The boat came up on top of the wave, with white water all around it. The oars were up, out of the water. For a second the boat began to turn on its side, then the oars went down into the water and the boat came down the side of the wave. Daniel could see the two people in the boat now. One was a man. One was a young woman.

He got up and ran down the rock. He was crying and laughing at the same time. 'It's all right, Mrs Dawson!' he shouted. 'It's all right! Look there! Look! Your angel is coming!'

10

Too Many People

Grace looked quickly behind her, and saw the people on the rock. They were waving, shouting, laughing. But there were eight, nine, perhaps ten of them! Too many for this small boat.

She looked back at the waves and pulled hard and carefully with her oars. It was more than a kilometre

For a second the boat began to turn on its side.

around the islands from the lighthouse to the ship, and every wave, every rock was different and dangerous. She was tired now, but the job was not finished. The wrecked ship on Harker's Rock was still fifty metres away.

'How many can you see, Grace?' her father shouted.

She looked again. 'Ten . . . twelve perhaps,' she said. 'It's too many, father. We'll all drown, if they try to get in.'

'Yes. Put me on the rock, lass, and then take the boat out again,' shouted William. 'I'll talk to them. We can't take more than five, the first time.'

It was very dangerous near the rock. In the best place, the waves went up and down two or three metres every minute. 'If we make one mistake,' Grace thought, 'the boat will break into fifty small pieces, and we'll be on the rock with the others.'

Carefully, slowly, Grace and her father tried to get the boat near the rock, but three times they had to pull away at the last minute. Then, the fourth time, William Darling jumped. The passengers pulled him onto the rock.

Grace quickly rowed the boat out to sea again. She was alone in the boat now, and the boat moved differently. She was tired, and her arms and back were hurting. But she knew about boats. 'Watch the sea all the time,' she told herself. 'The waves must meet the front of the boat first, or the boat will turn over. Forget the cold, and the rain, and the wet. God will help me.'

On the rock, William Darling spoke quickly. 'I'm going

to take the woman back with me,' he said. 'And that man there, with the broken leg. Then I need three strong men, to help me row the boat.' He looked at Daniel Donovan, and two others. 'You, man, and you, and you. The others must wait here. We'll come back for you later.'

'No, by God! Why me?' shouted James Kelly. 'I want to come now!'

'You're going to stay here, sir!' shouted William angrily. 'Don't you understand? If you get in the boat, we'll all drown!'

The fourth time, William Darling jumped.

'And my children,' cried Mrs Dawson, 'don't forget my children!'

William looked at her unhappily. He held out his arms. 'Give the children to me, mother,' he said.

Carefully, he took the boy and the girl from her, and put the little bodies on the rock, near the sea. They were dead and cold. 'They are in God's hands, mother,' he said. Then he spoke quickly and quietly to Daniel Donovan. 'When the boat comes, help me get the woman in. We can't take her children.'

Daniel agreed. William put his arm around Mrs Dawson, and waved to Grace.

Carefully, slowly, she rowed the boat in to the rock. It was harder without her father. The wind and the waves moved the boat more quickly, and Grace was very tired now. One mistake meant death for them all. She came closer – twenty metres, ten, seven, five . . . A big wave lifted the boat, then a smaller one behind it. She pulled hard on the oars, and threw a rope to a man on the rock. Then her father got into the boat, with a woman in his arms. She was screaming.

'My children! Bring the children, please!'

'No, mother.' William Darling took the oars. 'Help her, Grace.'

Grace went to the back of the boat with the woman, and held her. Daniel Donovan and two other men got in. They were carrying the man with the broken leg. The front of the boat was very near the rock now – too near.

Grace looked behind her, and saw a big wave.

'Pull, father!' she shouted. 'Pull hard!' She stood up, and pushed against the rock with an oar. The boat was very heavy now, with all these people in it.

William pulled hard with his oars. The big wave came in, and broke into white water all around them. But the boat did not hit the rock. William pulled again, and shouted. 'You men help me! Take the oars. One each!'

The little boat was very full. The sides were only just above the water, and often the water came in. Grace threw it out with her hat. The wind and waves were against them now, and the four men had to row hard. But slowly, very slowly, the lighthouse came nearer. At last, from the top

Slowly, very slowly, the lighthouse came nearer.

of the waves, they could see Thomasin Darling. She was standing in front of the lighthouse, and waving to them.

They were very tired when they got to the lighthouse. William and Daniel carried the man with the broken leg into the kitchen, and Grace and her mother helped Mrs Dawson.

Inside the kitchen, William smiled at his daughter. 'You did a good job, lass,' he said. 'Thank you.'

'I'll come back again with you, father,' she said.

'No,' he said. 'You're too tired. I'll take two of these.' He looked at Daniel and the other two men. 'Which are the strongest?' he asked.

Daniel was very tired. There was a fire in the kitchen – a warm, beautiful fire. He wanted to lie down in front of the fire and go to sleep for a long, long time. But William Darling's quiet brown eyes were looking at him.

'I'll come with you,' Daniel said.

'I'll come too,' said Thomas Buchanan.

William Darling smiled. 'Good men,' he said. 'Can you two men row as well as my daughter?'

Daniel looked at Grace, who was busy helping Mrs Dawson. She looked very small, here, in the kitchen – like any young woman. 'I'll try,' he said.

'Right,' said William. 'Come on then.'

So Daniel and Thomas Buchanan followed the old lighthouseman away from the warm kitchen fire, out into the rain and wind again. Daniel looked at the angry sea with its terrible waves, and he felt cold and frightened. He

Daniel wanted to lie down in front of the fire and go to sleep for a long, long time.

remembered the small young woman alone in the boat by Harker's Rock. 'Great God,' he thought. 'You made that girl strong, like an angel. Make me strong, too, like her.'

The Times   *London, 19th September 1838*

Mr Darling and his young daughter saved nine people from the wreck of the *Forfarshire*. The storm lasted for three days, and they stayed all that time with the Darlings in the lighthouse.

Queen Victoria thinks that Grace Darling is one of the finest young women in this country, and she is writing to thank her. One hundred years from now, people will remember this day.

GLOSSARY

angel a messenger from God, or a very special, wonderful person

blow (past tense **blew**) when air moves, a wind is 'blowing'

boot a heavy strong shoe that also covers the leg

broken *(adj)* in pieces or not working

can *(n)* a metal box

candle a stick of wax that gives light when it burns

captain the most important man on a ship

deck the floor on a ship

drown to die in water because you cannot breathe

engine a machine that makes a ship, car, etc. move

flash *(v)* to send out a sudden bright light

frightened *(adj)* very afraid

funnel a 'pipe' on top of a ship; smoke from the engine comes out of it

God the 'person' who made the world

great very big; or very important or special

hate the opposite of 'to love'

heroine (**hero**) a woman (man) who has done something brave or good

land *(n)* the part of the world that is not the sea

lantern a light in a glass box

lass a girl

lift *(v)* to take or move something up

lighthouse a tall building by the sea, with a strong light at night to tell ships about dangerous rocks

mainland land that is not an island

mirror a piece of glass that you can see yourself in

oar   a long piece of wood that you use to move a boat through water

oil *(n)*   a thick black liquid that you can burn

paddle wheel   a large wheel on the side of a ship that moves through the water

pray   to speak to God; to ask God for help

rock *(n)*   a very hard part of the ground

rocky   with a lot of rocks

rope *(n)*   very thick, strong string

row *(v)*   to move a boat with oars

save   to take someone out of danger

sir   a polite word for a man when you speak to him

stare *(v)*   to look hard at something for a long time

steam *(n)*   hot wet air; water changes into steam at 100°C

telescope   a long tube with special glass that makes things look bigger and nearer

throw (past tense **threw**)   to move something quickly through the air

tie *(v)*   to put ropes round something to hold it still

wave *(n)*   how the sea moves; a 'hill of water' in the sea

wave *(v)*   to move your hand through the air

wreck *(n)*   a broken ship; *(v)* to break something completely

Grace Darling

ACTIVITIES

44

ACTIVITIES

Before Reading

1 **Read the story introduction on the first page of the book, and the back cover. How much do you know now about the story? Tick one box for each sentence.**

		YES	NO
1	The story is true.	☐	☐
2	Grace Darling was a young man.	☐	☐
3	The story happened in 1838.	☐	☐
4	The *Forfarshire* was a ship.	☐	☐
5	The story happened off the north-east coast of Scotland.	☐	☐
6	It was a hot, dry night.	☐	☐
7	There was a wooden boat and an iron ship.	☐	☐
8	Some people were dying of cold on a rock.	☐	☐
9	Grace Darling was very frightened.	☐	☐
10	Grace Darling became famous.	☐	☐

2 **Which of these things can mean danger for a ship at sea? Explain why or why not.**

strong wind	fish	islands
blue skies	snow	very deep water
rocks	big waves	other big ships
sea birds	very hot sun	small sailing boats
heavy rain	storms	the dark

ACTIVITIES

While Reading

Read Chapter 1. On the ship Daniel Donovan starts to feel very afraid. Use these words from the story to complete the text. (Use each word once.)

angel, broken, dark, engines, frightened, happen, land, ship, stopped, waves, wind, worse

I feel very _____. The ship's _____ have _____ down and the big paddle wheels have _____.

The weather is getting _____ and it's nearly _____ now. We can't see the _____ any more. There is a very strong _____ and big _____ are hitting the side of the _____.

Everybody on the *Forfarshire* is afraid. We don't know what is going to _____. We need an _____ to save us!

Read Chapter 2, and then answer these questions.

1 Who was in the lighthouse that night?
2 Where were Grace's brothers?
3 How old were Grace, William and Thomasin?
4 What did William and Grace do to the lantern?
5 What was the lantern for?
6 If there was a shipwreck, what did William have to do?

Read Chapters 3 and 4. Here are some untrue sentences about them. Change them into true sentences.

1 The ship's engines were new.
2 The ship's engineer could mend the engines.
3 Daniel Donovan wanted the ship to stay at sea.
4 Grace never got up in the night to help her father.
5 They carried the oars into the kitchen.
6 William watched the light, and Grace went to bed.

Read Chapters 5 and 6. Who said this?

1 'I'm so frightened. Do you think we're going to die?'
2 'Rocks! There are rocks in front of us, rocks all round!'
3 'There's a ship on Harker's Rock.'
4 'I can see no one, but my eyes are old.'
5 'If there are people alive on that ship now, you cannot save them, William.'
6 'If there is someone alive, we can't just leave them to die.'

Read Chapters 7, 8 and 9. Choose the best question-word for these questions, and then answer them.

Why / Who / What
1 . . . prayed on the rock in a loud voice?
2 . . . did Daniel want everybody to do?
3 . . . was it difficult to stand at the top of the rock?
4 . . . first saw the people on the rock?

5 . . . was Grace angry?

6 . . . was the matter with Mrs Dawson's children?

7 . . . first saw the boat?

Before you read Chapter 10 (the title is *Too Many People*), can you guess what happens? Tick one box each time.

	YES	NO
1 Grace gets very tired and cannot row any more.	☐	☐
2 Grace falls into the sea and William pulls her back into the boat.	☐	☐
3 Mrs Dawson falls into the sea and drowns.	☐	☐
4 William and Grace can only take five people in the boat.	☐	☐
5 They leave Mrs Dawson's dead children on the rock.	☐	☐
6 The rest of the people on the rock die.	☐	☐
7 William takes the boat back a second time and saves more people.	☐	☐

Read Chapter 10, then answer these questions.

1 What did William and Grace do when they arrived at the rock?

2 Why did William need three strong men?

3 What did Grace use her hat for?

4 Who went back in the boat the second time?

5 How many people did William and Grace save?

ACTIVITIES

After Reading

1 **Thomasin Darling wrote a letter to her son William, telling him about the stormy night. Can you find and correct the twelve mistakes in it?**

The Lighthouse, Longstone Island

Dear William

I have so much to tell you! We have had a terrible storm here. It lasted for forty-eight hours, and the waves were more than two metres high!

A ship called the *Scotland* was wrecked on the beach. It was a small ship and it broke into four pieces. All of the passengers climbed onto Harker's Rock.

I was the first person to see the shipwreck and the passengers waving on the rock. Your father and Grace then got the boat out and rowed to the rock, but only four people could get in our little boat. The passengers did not help to row the boat back, and then your father and one other man went to the rock a second time and saved four more passengers.

Your sister Grace is now a famous heroine, and the King is writing to thank her – it's in all the newspapers!

Come home soon.

Love from Mother

2 Find the answers to this crossword in the story.

ACROSS

1 Grace watched the ship through a _____. (9)

4 The ship was going _____, from Hull to Dundee. (5)

6 The name of the ship. (11)

9 You row a boat with two of these. (4)

12 Daniel Donovan's job. (8)

13 Land which is not an island. (8)

14 To move a boat with oars. (3)

15 The ship was _____ in 1838. (7)

DOWN

2 The Darling family lived in this. (10)

3 Grace put _____ in the big lantern. (3)

5 Grace Darling was a famous _____. (7)

7 Daniel Donovan called Grace Darling an '_____'. (5)

8 A man who works on a ship. (6)

10 The floor on a ship. (4)

11 Longstone Island was one of the _____ Islands. (5)

3 **A reporter asked Daniel Donovan about the second journey to Harker's Rock. Complete their conversation. (Use as many words as you like.)**

REPORTER: What happened when you arrived at the lighthouse?

DANIEL: William Darling asked _____.

REPORTER: How did you feel about that?

DANIEL: I wanted _____ but _____.

REPORTER: So the two of you rowed back to Harker's Rock.

DANIEL: No, there _____.

REPORTER: Was the storm still bad?

DANIEL: Yes, the waves _____.

REPORTER: Were you afraid?

DANIEL: Very. But Grace Darling _____.

REPORTER: And what do you think of Grace Darling?

DANIEL: She's _____.

4 **William Darling took the woman and the man with the broken leg first. Imagine that you are saving people from a shipwreck, but your boat is small and you can only take four people. Which of these people do you save and why?**

1 A mother and her young child

2 A doctor (older woman)

3 A nurse (young man)

4 A bus-driver (older man)

5 A schoolboy (16 years old)

6 A famous film star (young woman)

7 A teacher (older woman)

8 A businessman (older man)

5 **Do you agree (A) or disagree (D) with these sentences? Explain why.**

1 The Captain of the *Forfarshire* was only doing his job. He wanted to take his ship and passengers to Scotland, and he was right not to go back to land.

2 Thomasin Darling didn't want Grace and William to go to the rock. She was right because it was a very stupid and dangerous thing to do.

3 Grace Darling was a famous heroine only because she was a young woman. William Darling, Daniel Donovan, and Thomas Buchanan were also heroes.

4 *Grace Darling* is not a special story. Grace and William Darling were only doing their jobs. People like firemen and policemen save people every day.

6 **Here are some different titles for the story. Which ones are good (G) and which are not good (NG)? Can you say why?**

Grace and William Darling	Heroine
The Angel from the Lighthouse	Shipwreck
The Captain Who Didn't Go Back	A Stormy Night
The End of the *Forfarshire*	Harker's Rock

ABOUT THE AUTHOR

Tim Vicary is an experienced teacher and writer, and has written several stories for the Oxford Bookworms Library. Many of these are in the Thriller & Adventure series, such as *White Death* (at Stage 1) or, like *Grace Darling*, in the True Stories series, such as *The Coldest Place on Earth* (also at Stage 1), which tells the story of the race between Scott and Amundsen to the South Pole. He has also published two long novels, *The Blood upon the Rose* and *Cat and Mouse*.

Tim Vicary has two children, and keeps dogs, cats, and horses. He lives and works in York, in the north of England.

ABOUT BOOKWORMS

OXFORD BOOKWORMS LIBRARY
Classics • True Stories • Fantasy & Horror • Human Interest
Crime & Mystery • Thriller & Adventure

The OXFORD BOOKWORMS LIBRARY offers a wide range of original and adapted stories, both classic and modern, which take learners from elementary to advanced level through six carefully graded language stages:

Stage 1 (400 headwords)	**Stage 4** (1400 headwords)
Stage 2 (700 headwords)	**Stage 5** (1800 headwords)
Stage 3 (1000 headwords)	**Stage 6** (2500 headwords)

More than fifty titles are also available on cassette, and there are many titles at Stages 1 to 4 which are specially recommended for younger learners. In addition to the introductions and activities in each Bookworm, resource material includes photocopiable test worksheets and Teacher's Handbooks, which contain advice on running a class library and using cassettes, and the answers for the activities in the books.

Several other series are linked to the OXFORD BOOKWORMS LIBRARY. They range from highly illustrated readers for young learners, to playscripts, non-fiction readers, and unsimplified texts for advanced learners.

Oxford Bookworms Starters	*Oxford Bookworms Factfiles*
Oxford Bookworms Playscripts	*Oxford Bookworms Collection*

Details of these series and a full list of all titles in the OXFORD BOOKWORMS LIBRARY can be found in the *Oxford English* catalogues. A selection of titles from the OXFORD BOOKWORMS LIBRARY can be found on the next pages.

BOOKWORMS · TRUE STORIES · STAGE 2

The Death of Karen Silkwood

JOYCE HANNAM

This is the story of Karen Silkwood. It begins with her death.

Why does her story begin where it should end? Certain people wanted her death to be an ending. Why? What were they afraid of? Karen Silkwood had something to tell us, and she believed that it was important. Why didn't she live to tell us? Will we ever know what really happened? The questions go on and on, but there are no answers.

This is a true story. It happened in Oklahoma, USA, where Karen Silkwood lived and worked . . . and died.

BOOKWORMS · TRUE STORIES · STAGE 2

The Love of a King

PETER DAINTY

All he wanted to do was to marry the woman he loved. But his country said 'No!'

He was Edward VIII, King of Great Britain, King of India, King of Australia, and King of thirty-nine other countries. And he loved the wrong woman.

She was beautiful and she loved him – but she was already married to another man.

It was a love story that shook the world. The King had to choose: to be King, or to have love . . . and leave his country, never to return.

BOOKWORMS · CRIME & MYSTERY · STAGE 2

Sherlock Holmes Short Stories

SIR ARTHUR CONAN DOYLE

Retold by Clare West

Sherlock Holmes is the greatest detective of them all. He sits in his room, and smokes his pipe. He listens, and watches, and thinks. He listens to the steps coming up the stairs; he watches the door opening – and he knows what question the stranger will ask.

In these three of his best stories, Holmes has three visitors to the famous flat in Baker Street – visitors who bring their troubles to the only man in the world who can help them.

BOOKWORMS · HUMAN INTEREST · STAGE 2

Stories from the Five Towns

ARNOLD BENNETT

Retold by Nick Bullard

Arnold Bennett is famous for his stories about the Five Towns and the people who live there. They look and sound just like other people, and, like all of us, sometimes they do some very strange things. There's Sir Jee, who is a rich businessman. So why is he making a plan with a burglar? Then there is Toby Hall. Why does he decide to visit Number 11 Child Row, and who does he find there? And then there are the Hessian brothers and Annie Emery – and the little problem of twelve thousand pounds.

BOOKWORMS • TRUE STORIES • STAGE 2

William Shakespeare

JENNIFER BASSETT

William Shakespeare. Born April 1564, at Stratford-upon-Avon. Died April 1616. Married Anne Hathaway: two daughters, one son. Actor, poet, famous playwright. Wrote nearly forty plays.

But what was he like as a man? What did he think about when he rode into London for the first time . . . or when he was writing his plays *Hamlet* and *Romeo and Juliet* . . . or when his only son died?

We know the facts of his life, but we can only guess at his hopes, his fears, his dreams.

BOOKWORMS • TRUE STORIES • STAGE 3

The Brontë Story

TIM VICARY

On a September day in 1821, in the church of a Yorkshire village, a man and six children stood around a grave. They were burying a woman: the man's wife, the children's mother. The children were all very young, and within a few years the two oldest were dead, too.

Close to the wild beauty of the Yorkshire moors, the father brought up his young family. Who had heard of the Brontës of Haworth then? Branwell died while he was still a young man, but the three sisters who were left had an extraordinary gift. They could write marvellous stories – *Jane Eyre*, *Wuthering Heights*, *The Tenant of Wildfell Hall* . . . But Charlotte, Emily, and Anne Brontë did not live to grow old or to enjoy their fame. Only their father was left, alone with his memories.